TOGETHER, a FOREST

Drawing Connections Between Nature's Diversity and Our Own

Roz MacLean

Henry Holt and Company

New York

Today, a field trip to the forest!

An ecosystem is made up of all the living and nonliving things in an area.

Joy recites to herself. She always pays attention in class.

Ms. Khan hands out sketchbooks. "The forest is big," she says, "so pick one thing for our art project. Choose whatever you feel *drawn* to."

Joy takes in the wild all around her.
How will she know the right
thing to choose?

Hakim starts exploring right away, just like Salal,
whose zigzagging branches wander the forest floor,
zinging into bright pink and white flowers.

Hakim's mind zigzags too—between curiosities,
noticings, and juicy new discoveries!

Sasha pauses from walking with her white cane to listen
to the birds. Their calls sound different as they move behind
branches or farther away, and the trees and plants create
sound shadows.

It all helps her to understand her surroundings.
She presses record and wonders, *What are they saying?*

Ben wants to wrap himself up in Moss like a blanket. Little stems and leaves sponge up moisture from the air and hold on to mist, like memories to be shared later. Just like Ben's supersponge memory that absorbs every fact about dinosaurs (Ben LOVES dinosaurs).

Angel can't find the colored pencil she
needs from her collection. Caught up
in the moment, she often forgets or
misplaces things.

Squirrel might not always remember where
he buries his seeds come wintertime, but he
gathers so many that he plants much more than
he needs. This way, he'll still have enough to
eat, and some will grow into trees!

There it is! Angel remembers how
much she likes drawing fluffy tails.

Lichens remind Sofia of bursts of electricity, like what makes her power wheelchair zoom. Lichens thrive because at least two beings work together: fungi and algae.

Fungi give Lichens their shape, while algae make food from the sun. Sofia's life is full of teamwork and helping too.

Alex hears a buzz whizz by their ear. Bee is thrilled to visit her flower neighbors! She zooms through the air from one flower friend to the next.

Alex never wants to stop moving either, like they have a motor! They want to visit all of their friends!

The Creek is thrumming after a big rain. In drier times, it will be shallow, slow, or still. Akash feels like the changing stream, with emotions that can be big, crashing, and even overflow.

Other times, he might feel more low, quiet, or steady. It all flows onto his page.

Diwa feels the wind from the
Waterfall move through her body,
shimmering into her happy, dancing hands.
Ferns flutter in the mist, joining her excitement.

The ways she moves her body—like jumping, clapping, rocking, and humming—help her feel "just right."

Joy feels all wrong. Everyone else is choosing, but she has no idea what she feels drawn to. How is she supposed to know?

Nisha has found Mushrooms. Below the ground's surface, they send out tiny threads—mycelium—to join with other roots and create a giant web. The web helps plants get all the nutrition from the soil, share food with one another, and communicate like they're talking on the phone!

Nisha wants everyone to be okay, and she
can feel when things are unfair. She loves
that when she is with others, they can
make up a web of caring too.

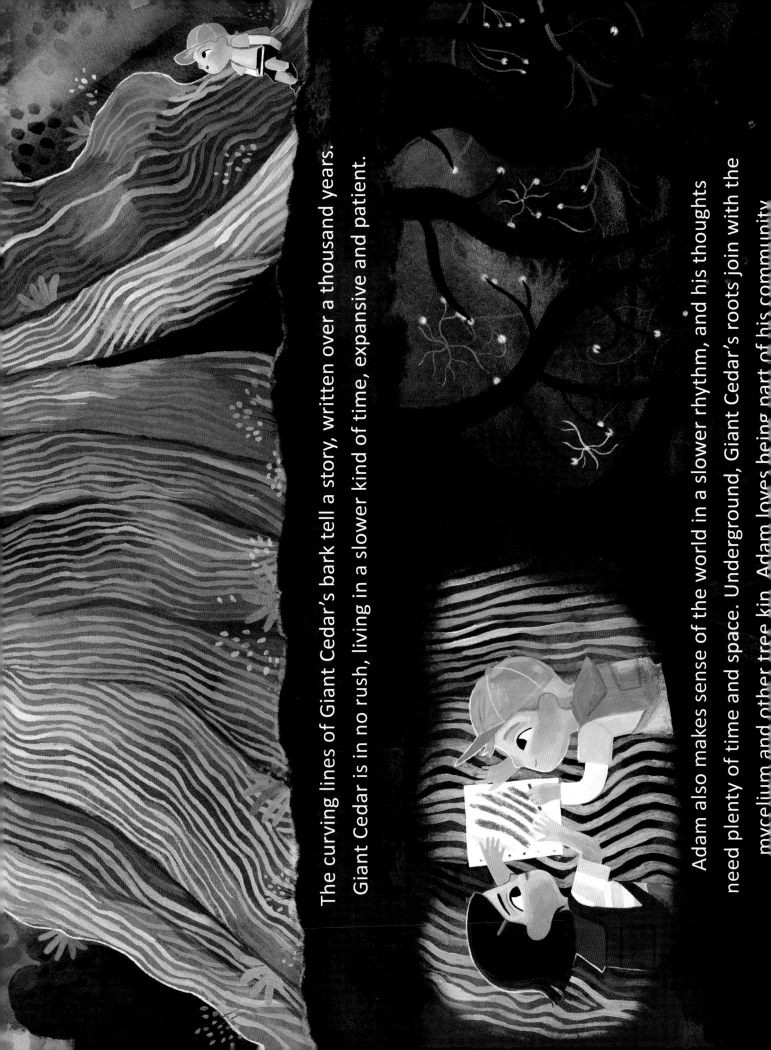

The curving lines of Giant Cedar's bark tell a story, written over a thousand years. Giant Cedar is in no rush, living in a slower kind of time, expansive and patient.

Adam also makes sense of the world in a slower rhythm, and his thoughts need plenty of time and space. Underground, Giant Cedar's roots join with the mycelium and other tree kin. Adam loves being part of his community.

Covered in moss and lichen, Bigleaf Maple is not a writer like Giant Cedar, but an inventor! They designed their seeds to fly like helicopters so they can find a good place to grow.

Manuel is also a creative. Even though reading and writing isn't easy for him, he is always dreaming up new solutions and ideas.

Lucas—swept up in spinning thoughts and memories—stops when he notices Turkey Tail. The fungi are breaking down deadwood and becoming vibrant works of art!

As he draws, his thoughts and worries find their way onto the paper. He can imagine beautiful new colors and forms too!

Tree Frog appears still, but her glossy skin is busy absorbing water from the air and might even change from green to brown. It depends on her senses and how light, dark, cool, warm, dry, or wet her surroundings are.

Amir has keen senses too. Sound, touch, and how things feel on his skin can be intense. He loves when light twinkles gently through leaves, but other times light can feel harsh.

He doesn't always notice what's going on *inside* his body, and he wonders if Tree Frog feels it when she changes color.

HOP!

Away she goes to find a more perfect spot.

The morning is almost done, and Joy still hasn't found her part of the forest to draw. Is this her first failed assignment?

Then, a glimmer of purple turns her head.
A small flower, so lovely it sings to her heart. *So beautiful*, she thinks.

But she isn't looking where she's going and doesn't see the root and—

SPLASH!

Hakim notices right away.

Nisha says something to Alex, who zooms off to tell the others.

Do you want a squeeze?

Are you feeling okay?

She shakes her head no.

Joy does, and it helps.

I can take your bag.

Remember, slow breaths.

Thanks.

Of course! We're a team.

She exhales slowly.

At the picnic area, Ben has dry clothes waiting for her.
He's always prepared.

She didn't, but the fact makes her smile.

After she changes, she sits in the warm spot Amir has saved
for her to dry off. Nisha has gathered a hodgepodge for her
lunch made up of everyone's extras. Tasty!

On the bus, Sasha plays her recording of birdsongs.

What do you think dinosaurs sounded like?

Probably Tweet, tweet . . . CHOMP! CHOMP!

Manuel's hands bite into Joy's shoulders like teeth.

In class, inspired by Lucas's and Akash's drawings, Joy draws her flower from memory.

That's so pretty.

Ms. Khan agrees. "I think your flower is an Orchid. Their seeds start out so tiny that they don't have any food stored. Fungi living nearby help them grow by sharing nutrition, and when the Orchid gets bigger, they give back food to the fungi. Orchids need just the right conditions, so when they bloom, it's a good sign for the whole ecosystem."

Joy thinks of all the help she has gotten from another ecosystem—
her classmates. Her heart feels full.

She can feel how much she counts on them.

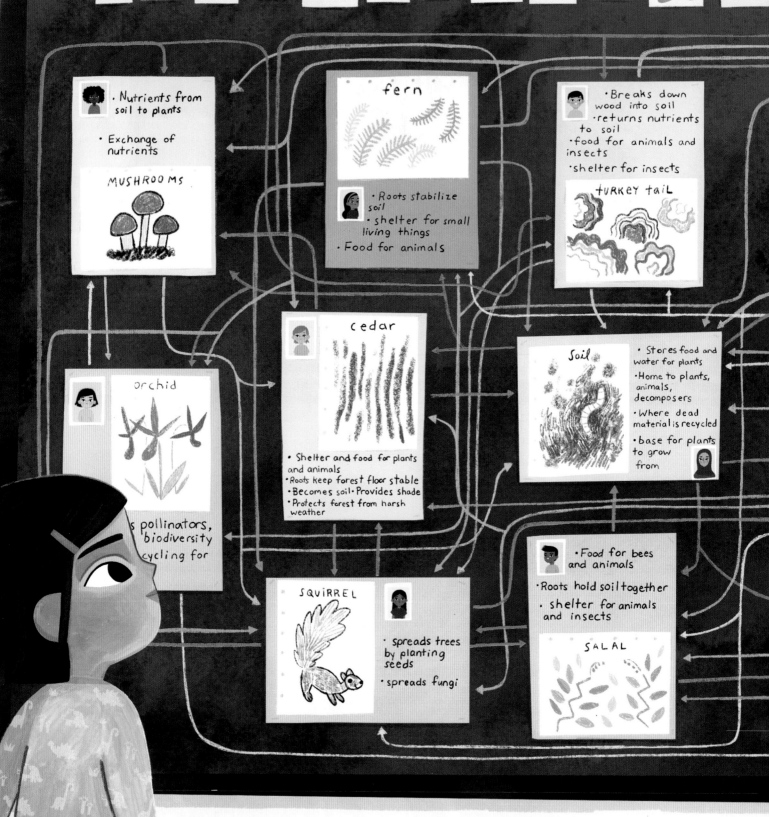

OUR CLASS

- Nutrients from soil to plants
- Exchange of nutrients

MUSHROOMS

fern
- Roots stabilize soil
- shelter for small living things
- Food for animals

- Breaks down wood into soil
- returns nutrients to soil
- food for animals and insects
- shelter for insects

TURKEY TAIL

cedar
- Shelter and food for plants and animals
- Roots keep forest floor stable
- Becomes soil • Provides shade
- Protects forest from harsh weather

Soil
- Stores food and water for plants
- Home to plants, animals, decomposers
- Where dead material is recycled
- base for plants to grow from

orchid
s pollinators,
biodiversity
cycling for

SQUIRREL
- spreads trees by planting seeds
- spreads fungi

- Food for bees and animals
- Roots hold soil together
- shelter for animals and insects

SALAL

How much they all count on each other.